Dancing with the Stars

"*I think you ought to audition for the Junior Associates, Jasmine. That would mean going to Covent Garden in London, and doing the junior Royal Ballet class every Saturday,*" *said Miss Coralie.*

A big gasp rushed out of me. "*Royal Ballet! But am I good enough?*"

Ballerina Dreams

Collect all the books in the series:

Poppy's Secret Wish

Jasmine's Lucky Star

Rose's Big Decision

Dancing Princess

Dancing For Ever

Ballerina Dreams

Dancing with the Stars

Ann Bryant

USBORNE

For Amy Hollingworth, a truly wonderful dancer,
and my inspiration for the character of Anna Lane.

My thanks, also, to Elizabeth Old, Artistic Coordinator
of the Rambert Dance Company, and to all the Rambert
dancers. Watching your class was the best research
I've ever had to do!

The publisher would like to thank Sara Matthews of
the Central School of Ballet for her assistance.

First published in the UK in 2005 by Usborne Publishing Ltd.,
Usborne House, 83-85 Saffron Hill, London EC1N 8RT, England.
www.usborne.com

Copyright © 2005 by Ann Bryant

A CPI catalogue record for this title is available
from the British Library.

JF AMJJASOND/05
ISBN 0 7460 6434 9

Printed in Great Britain.

1 The Magic Moment

Hi! I'm Jasmine. I'm feeling on top of the world because I've just had a "lovely" from Miss Coralie, my ballet teacher. She's a very strict teacher with incredibly high standards, so when you get a "lovely" you really feel honoured. Miss Coralie used to dance with the Royal Ballet, before starting the Coralie Charlton School of Ballet, which is where my friends Poppy and Rose and I all go. It's the best dancing school around. Rose is on grade four, and that's brilliant considering she only started ballet lessons a year and two terms ago, and Poppy and I are on grade five.

This hour from five thirty till six thirty on a Tuesday is my favourite hour of the week. I'm always dreaming about it when I'm supposed to be concentrating on my school work. My dad would be really cross if he knew that, because he thinks ballet is nothing compared to school work, but to me, it's everything. And I'm really sad that it's the last ballet lesson of term today and then we've got three weeks without lessons over the Easter holidays.

"Moving on to steps, girls," said Miss Coralie. "Let's try *pas de bourrée, pas de bourrée, assemblé, assemblé...*" Miss Coralie showed us by marking it through, which means doing it roughly. She uses her hands too, when she's marking. I love this part of the lesson, when we have to remember a sequence of steps and do it straight away, especially when I'm in the front row, like I am now, and I have to make my brain work really fast.

"Right, one row at a time," said Miss Coralie briskly. "Start in fifth position, *demi-plié* and..." Mrs. Marsden, the pianist, played a bar of music for us to prepare. "Point those toes harder, girls, and close in tighter... Turn out the supporting leg. Lift up out of the ribs..."

I felt as though Miss Coralie was a hawk watching its prey, the way her eyes bored into me. She didn't seem to be paying quite the same amount of attention to anyone else, so when it was the next row's turn to do the sequence I quickly looked down to check that my drawstrings were tucked into my shoes. She's very particular about our uniform. We have to look totally neat and tidy all the time.

Maybe my tights have got a dirty mark on them, I thought, when Miss Coralie was still staring at my ankles during the *révérence*. I tried to look down, but it was impossible without lowering my head, and your chin is supposed to be tilted slightly up during this final curtsey, as if you're looking out to the audience at the end of a ballet, and thanking everyone for watching. That's what Miss Coralie says anyway.

Every time I do the *révérence* I imagine that it really is the end of a ballet and that I'm one of the soloists at a big theatre in London, like Covent Garden or Sadler's Wells. I've been to both those theatres and I absolutely love them. I've even been backstage at Sadler's Wells and met one of the dancers, Anna Lane. It all happened because Poppy and Rose and I all won a prize at Miss Coralie's show and the adjudicator, Miss Bird, invited us to go to London to watch her daughter, Anna, dancing. It was one of the best times of my life, especially meeting Anna afterwards. She's such a nice, friendly person as well as being my favourite dancer. And I've met Miss Bird lots of times now because my mum is on the same fund-raising committee as her, and they sometimes meet at our house. Even if they meet somewhere else, my mum always comes home and says that Miss Bird sent her love or asked how my ballet was going.

"Jasmine, can I have a word with you, please?"

I came back to earth with a jolt at the sound of Miss Coralie's voice.

Poppy turned to me with big eyes. I think she was as puzzled as I was. Miss Coralie doesn't usually keep anyone back after class unless it's about something quite important. Everyone went out to the changing room except Tamsyn Waters. She was fiddling with her ballet shoes but there was nothing wrong with them. I'm sure she was just hanging around so she could hear what Miss Coralie wanted to say to me. But Miss Coralie was talking to Mrs. Marsden for ages while I stood there, and in the end Tamsyn had to go.

When Miss Coralie turned round her face

was serious. "Jasmine, we need to think about your ballet future. You're doing so well, but to make real progress at this stage, you should be doing more than one class per week."

My first thought was: *More ballet! Brilliant!* But then there quickly came a little tug of worry. If Miss Coralie had said what she'd just said a year ago, my spirits would have sunk down through the floorboards because my dad would never have let me do the extra lessons in a million years. You see, he's a doctor and he really disapproves of ballet because of stretching and pushing your body into unnatural shapes. Unfortunately, no matter what I say about how it's good for you too, he refuses to believe me. Also, out of every single one of my friends' fathers, I've got the strictest one. He thinks that school work and getting high marks in exams are all that matter. He keeps telling me that people only get good jobs in law and medicine and things if they work really hard at school. But I don't want a job like that. All I want is to be a ballerina. That's my dream.

My dad used to say that I had to give up ballet when I started secondary school, which is in five months' time, but he completely changed his mind when he saw me dance in Miss Coralie's show. I'll never forget the look in his eyes when I spotted him in the audience clapping and clapping. He seemed so very proud.

I shook the little tug of worry away. There wasn't a problem any more. And with Miss Coralie's next words the very last anxious little puff turned into a truly magic moment.

"I think you ought to audition for the Junior Associates, Jasmine. That would mean going to Covent Garden in London, and doing the junior Royal Ballet class every Saturday."

A big gasp rushed out of me. "Royal Ballet! But am I good enough?"

Miss Coralie smiled. "I wouldn't be suggesting it if I didn't think you were up to standard, Jasmine."

"I'd really *really* love to audition," I said in scarcely more than a whisper, my mouth felt so dry with excitement. "Even if I don't get in, it'd be so brilliant just to audition."

"You've got a jolly good chance of getting in, Jasmine. But we can cross that bridge when we come to it. I'll be receiving the information about dates and places for the auditions at the end of April or the beginning of May, so we've got a few weeks yet. I just wanted to find out how you felt about the idea at this stage."

"I feel over the moon," I said.

"That's great. Shall I leave you to ask your parents then?"

That tiny tug of worry was back. Might it be better if Miss Coralie asked them? I wasn't sure, but I nodded anyway.

She looked at me carefully. "Good."

✳

As soon as I got into the changing room, Poppy grabbed both my hands and raised her eyebrows.

Tamsyn was talking but she stopped when she saw me and spoke in her *not-really-interested* voice. "So what did Miss Coralie want?"

I suddenly felt a bit shy about saying it out loud because the whole changing room was silent, waiting for me to speak, and I didn't want to sound at all showy-offy.

"Erm...she thinks I ought to audition for the Royal Ballet Saturday classes," I said very quietly.

"Oh, that's so cool, Jazz!" said Poppy, jumping up and down, and clutching my wrists. Then everyone was congratulating me.

Tamsyn started looking in her bag again. I noticed she waited till it went quiet before she spoke. "Mum said that's what *I'm* probably going to do, actually."

"Wow! You lucky thing!" said Sophie. "I wish *I* was as talented as you two."

"How come you didn't mention that before, Tamsyn?" asked Immy.

"In case Jasmine felt bad," replied Tamsyn. Then she turned right round to look at me. "Because your dad probably won't let you do the audition, will he?"

Her words felt like big punches in my stomach. And then my mind started arguing with itself.

What if she's right and my dad won't let me do it?

No, that's silly. Of course he'll let me. He's been totally fine about my ballet lessons ever since the show.

But this is different. Saturday lessons at Royal Ballet means you're very serious about ballet.

Papa doesn't know that I want it to be my career though, does he?

All the same, it would take up most of Saturday with the journey and he won't be happy about that.

But it's only an audition and it's not for ages. What was it Miss Coralie said? "We can cross that bridge when we come to it." Yes, it's probably better not to say anything until we at least know the date. In fact, maybe I'll ask Miss Coralie to tell my dad about it first.

That's when the thoughts in my head stopped, and I realized Poppy was standing right beside me. We waited till everyone had gone back to their conversations, then, keeping our hands by our sides, we pressed our thumbs against each other's. It's called a thumb-thumb and it's what we do for good luck. As our thumbs pressed together, I thought the very words that Poppy whispered under her breath, just loudly enough for me to hear.

Please let him say yes.

2 An Important Meeting

After ballet my mum dropped me off at the library, which stays open late on Tuesdays, while she went to the supermarket. I love it at the library, especially in the arts section. I found a really good book about choreography and couldn't wait till Poppy and Rose broke up for the holidays so I could show them.

I've already broken up because I go to a different school from them. It's going to be so great when we can spend all day dancing together. Luckily, my mum isn't anywhere near as strict as my dad. Otherwise, she'd make me do piano practice or extra homework for my tutor or something. I wish I could give up piano because I'm supposed to practise for at least twenty minutes every day and it gets in the way of my ballet.

"Ready to go, *chérie*?"

It was my mum. She calls me "*chérie*" because she's French. I've always used the French names for Mum and Dad, which are Maman and Papa, even though my dad's Egyptian. I hadn't even noticed Maman coming in, I'd been so wrapped up in my thoughts.

She went rushing on ahead when we were out of the library. "The car's still in the supermarket car park."

I trailed behind because I was trying to read my book.

"Hurry up, Jasmeen. I've got lots to do this evening while Papa's away."

Papa's often away. He's a doctor and a

surgeon and he has to go to conferences and things, sometimes abroad.

I snapped my book shut and that's when it happened. I looked up and saw *her*. I was sure it was her. Driving a little blue car that was just turning into the car park.

"Look!"

"What?"

"Isn't that...?"

"Jasmeen!"

I was the one rushing ahead now, because I was convinced I'd just seen Anna Lane. "Look, she's turning into the car park. Quick, Maman!"

"Who?"

"Anna!"

I'd gone way ahead of Maman and I could see the blue car pulling into a space at one end of the car park.

"Where are you going? Our car's over here, Jasmeen!" Maman called frantically.

"I want to see if it's her…" I called back.

Maman started to hurry off towards the car. "And *I* want to get home."

The door of the blue car was opening so I stood still about twenty metres away and watched. A second later, I knew I'd been right. It was Anna. I didn't even have to see her face – I could tell by the way she moved with her totally straight, slim back. And now she was locking the car and hurrying with beautiful turned-out feet towards the supermarket. It seemed so weird seeing her in this ordinary little town when I always imagined her leading a glamorous dancer's life in London. Of course, I knew she must come to visit her mother, Miss Bird, but I'd never actually come across her shopping or anything before. I wanted to say hello, but I'd suddenly turned shy. Just because I'd met her didn't mean she was my friend. I couldn't just shout out: *Anna!* But then I mustn't let myself miss this chance of talking to my favourite dancer. She might be going straight back to London when she'd done her shopping.

For goodness' sake, call out to her! I told myself crossly, as I watched her getting further and further away.

"Jasmeen, come on!" That was my *mum's* cross voice.

"I just want to say hello…"

"Well she's gone inside now and you can't go chasing after her when she's not at the theatre. Hurry up, Jasmeen, I'm running late."

We walked to the car and I got in slowly. We were just pulling away when I saw Anna coming out of the supermarket.

"Stop!"

Maman slammed on the brakes. "What? What?"

"She's there! Look!"

Anna was hurrying back to the car with a bit of an anxious look on her face.

"Jasmeen! I thought I was about to run someone over, the way you yelled out like that!"

"Oh, *please* come with me, Maman. Just to say hello." I put my praying hands right under her nose. "*Please!*"

She pulled into the nearest space with a sharp sigh and we both got out.

"Anna!" I didn't care about calling out any more.

She looked round and I saw that anxious look again in her eyes, but it was gone in a flash. "Jasmine! Hello. What a surprise. I'm just getting a few bits for Mum, but I left my list in the car."

"This is *my* mum." I felt shy introducing Maman to a famous person.

"Hello, I'm Sylvie," said Maman, shaking hands. "I know your mother very well. We sit on the same committee."

Anna smiled, but she still looked a bit

frazzled. "I'm so sorry to have to rush away, when I've only just met you, but I'm trying to sort everything out for Mum before I go back to London tomorrow. I've been looking after her for a few days because she's had a virus. But I've absolutely got to get back for class and rehearsals tomorrow."

I tried to imagine how Anna must have been feeling. I knew that professional dancers did a class every single day. I've always wished I could watch one.

"Oh dear..." said Maman. "I had no idea poor Bridget hasn't been well. I'll pop in and see her."

"That's very kind of you." Anna smiled. "I'm sure she'd love to have visitors now she's back on her feet. I'm just so relieved that she's all right to leave now because we're going on tour in a few weeks and I'm desperately needed for rehearsals of the new pieces."

I loved listening to Anna talking like this.

It was so brilliant to catch a little glimpse of the wonderful world of professional dancing. "So how have they managed the new dances without you?" I asked her.

"Well, they've just had to do the best they can." She smiled at me. "You know what it's like when you're working up to a show, Jasmine."

I nodded hard. "I love shows! And I love class too! I bet one of your classes would be amazing. I'd love to see one. I can't wait till I'm a professional dancer." Then, before I knew it, I'd blurted out the very thing I'd decided not to mention yet. "And guess what! Miss Coralie wants me to audition for the Junior Associates of the Royal Ballet!"

"Oh!" said Maman, blinking a bit.

"Wow!" said Anna, at exactly the same time. "That's fantastic news, Jasmine!"

"It's not for ages..." I said, looking at Maman, and feeling a bit embarrassed in case she was wondering why I hadn't mentioned it before. "I wasn't going to tell Papa until we know the date," I added quietly.

She nodded then, and her lips went a bit tight. I knew what she was thinking.

When I looked back at Anna, I saw that she was frowning. No wonder. She must have thought it was a bit weird that I didn't want to tell my dad straight away.

"Well anyway..." she said, looking at her watch. But then she looked back at me with that same frown, as though she was trying to work something out. Her eyes took in my jeans and T-shirt. "Are you on school holidays at the moment?"

I nodded. "We broke up last Friday."

"Are you doing anything tomorrow?"

A lovely tremble of excitement was starting in my stomach, but I wasn't sure why. I looked at Maman.

"No particular plans, no," she said, shaking her head.

"In that case," said Anna, "would you like to come to London and watch my class? It's classical ballet, so it might inspire you when it comes to your audition."

I gave a massive gasp. I thought I must have died and gone to heaven. I would be watching real professional dancers doing a class. "Oh, yes! I'd absolutely love to! Can I, Maman?"

"Well, that's a very kind offer, Anna..."

"So that means I can, doesn't it!"

"Well, if you're sure, Anna..."

"Quite sure!"

"Thank you, thank you, thank you!" I couldn't help crying out at the top of my voice.

"Ssh!" said Maman. "Not in public, Jasmeen!"

But I didn't care.

3 On the Way

On the way back home from the supermarket, all I wanted to talk about was the next day. We'd arranged what time to meet Anna at the station and we'd sorted out how I'd get home. Maman said that Papa was working in a London hospital all through the night and coming home the next day at lunchtime, so he'd probably be able to pick me up and bring me home in the car. But I was still a little bit anxious, just in case he said I couldn't go. Only a teeny bit though, because Maman seemed to think it would be fine. So then I got all excited again, gabbling on about how brilliant it was going to be.

"I wonder what the dancers will wear."

Maman was frowning, and at first I thought she was trying to picture all the dancers, but I was wrong.

"So Miss Coralie said you could audition for the Junior Royal Ballet?"

My heart started racing. "Yes, but it's not for ages…" I pretended to be suddenly very interested in something out of the window and I was glad Maman was driving so she couldn't see my anxious face. I didn't want her to think the auditions were very important, otherwise she'd tell Papa, and I was sure in my mind now that it would be best if Miss Coralie talked to him about it first.

"Hmm," said Maman. "And if you *did* audition and you were accepted, what then?"

I kept looking out of the window. Half of me wanted to tell her in a big excited rush about going to Covent Garden every Saturday, but the other half wanted to pretend it wasn't very important at all so that she wouldn't tell Papa. In the end I decided to tell the truth.

"It would mean going to class in London on Saturdays," I said carefully. Then I turned to face her and spoke in my urgent voice. "But Miss Coralie's going to tell you about it when she knows the date so please don't tell Papa, will you?"

Maman flicked her head to look at me for a second. "Oh, right. Miss Coralie will let us know?"

"Yes," I said, nodding, and realized then that I'd been sitting up straight all that time, pushing against the seat belt, so I flopped back, with a lovely feeling of relief and went back onto my cloud of happiness, thinking about the next day.

As soon as we got home I went on the Internet

to look at the Rambert Dance Company site. That's Anna's company. I'd seen it lots of times before, but I love looking at the pictures and reading all about them. Then I went into the Royal Ballet School site. It said that the Junior Associates' auditions would be announced shortly, and that made me so excited I had to get up and dance around my room and out on the landing and back in my room again. I reminded myself of Rose when I did that. That's exactly the kind of mad thing she would do.

When Papa phoned at eight o'clock, Maman answered and I sat at the table with my fists pressed against my mouth, and a little prayer going on inside me.

Please let him say I can go to Anna's class.

She spoke to him for at least two minutes before she handed me the phone, smiling. "It's okay," she mouthed.

And it was. "It's worked out very well!" said

Papa, when I'd told him how excited I was. "I'm working at a hospital not far from the Rambert studios, so I can pick you up after the class and we can both come home together."

He sounded in such a good mood that I was really tempted to tell him about the Junior Associates after all. But I knew I wouldn't be able to bear it if he said I wasn't allowed to audition, and I didn't want anything to spoil my lovely feeling about watching Anna's class, so I kept quiet. I still had some homework to finish but I could hardly concentrate at all and I knew it was going to be impossible to get to sleep that night.

The next morning, I leaped out of bed feeling like the luckiest girl in the world. Maman took me to the station, and Anna was already there. After Maman had gone we stood on the platform together and while we were waiting for the train, Anna exercised her ankles, turning each one very slowly. I could see her shoulders moving a bit too.

"I can't wait to get back into the swing," she said. "It's not poor Mum's fault, but this is a really bad time for me to be taking days off, with the tour coming up, especially when I'm in all four of the new dances."

"So do you just dance the four new pieces every night when you're on tour?"

"We've got two programmes – one for Monday, Wednesday and Friday evening performances, and one for Tuesdays and Thursdays. We dance four pieces in each programme, two old and two new."

I wanted to shout out to everyone that the famous Anna Lane was talking to little *me*. But then she looked suddenly worried. "Where *is* this train? I mustn't be late."

And at that very second it chugged into view. We couldn't find seats together because it was so crowded, so we sat diagonally opposite each other. I kept watching people to see if they realized there was a famous ballerina in the carriage with them. But I suppose being a ballerina is nothing like being a pop star. You hardly ever see pictures of ballerinas, and it would be impossible to recognize them, even if you did, because when they're dancing on stage they've got their hair scraped back or they're wearing a headdress, and they've always got lots of make-up on.

Anna had taken her trainers off and tucked one leg underneath her. She was reading a book, so I started reading too because we couldn't talk without people listening. I could tell she was still a bit anxious about the time though because she kept on looking at her watch whenever the train slowed down. I could see the toes of one foot wiggling around inside her sock and I guessed she was doing exercises. Her back was completely straight and just her head tipped forwards to read the book.

On the Way

When we got to London we rushed down escalators and along corridors in the underground. Anna flew past everybody like a silent streak with me right next to her. I've never known a grown-up be able to move so fast without getting puffed out. We came to the platform we needed and a train was already there with the doors open. Anna grabbed my hand and we plunged on just before the doors shut. I felt like giggling with the excitement but Anna was looking worried again.

"Are you nervous about class?" I asked her quietly.

She smiled. "No, quite the opposite! I'm desperate to be back with the music and the atmosphere and everything. I've got a *barre* at Mum's, so I've practised every day, but it's not the same. I'm nervous about being late, though. It's disrespectful to the teacher. Most people turn up early and do some stretching before class."

It was incredible. Anna was actually worrying about what the teacher would say if she walked into class late. That's exactly like me and Poppy and Rose. Miss Coralie is very strict about timing and behaviour as well as uniform. And no one talks from the moment we queue up outside till we're back in the corridor after class.

"I can't wait to see what you do!" I said, hugging myself, then nearly losing my balance as the train lurched to a halt.

Anna laughed. "It'll be just like one of your classes, I expect."

Only much harder, I thought to myself.

I went into a bit of a daydream for the rest of the journey, wondering what Anna's teacher was going to look like, but I gave up trying to imagine her in the end because I could only get pictures of Miss Coralie in my head.

When we came out of the underground, we had to walk quite a long way, but Anna kept on breaking into a jog. I was wearing my jogging bottoms and trainers, so it felt kind of right. We passed the hospital where I thought Papa was working, then after a few minutes we stopped outside a tall building with *Rambert Dance Company* written across it in big white letters.

"Here we are!" said Anna, keying in a code on the panel beside the door.

My heart beat faster. "I can't believe I'm here!" I said in a bit of a squeaky whisper.

Anna smiled and we went in.

4 The Ballet Teacher

"That's one of the studios." Anna was pointing to a big hall on the left. "But we prefer to do class in the other studio at the top because it's lighter and brighter."

I caught a glimpse of mirrors before I was shooting upstairs after her.

"This is the reception," she told me quickly.

"Hi, Anna!" two or three people called out.

On the next floor, she pushed open a door. "This is the changing room." It was very messy, with *pointe* shoes and clothes everywhere, even though there were lots of tall metal lockers. All over the walls, there were hooks with towels and clothes and ballet shoes hanging from them. "Shan't be a sec, Jasmine."

I couldn't help staring, because when Poppy and I get changed we always have to make sure we're completely neat and clean in our leotards and tights with not a millimetre of pants showing, and with our hair tied back in a bun with a hairband rounding it all off. But Anna just flung her jumper and jeans on the floor and put on a vest top with a sweatshirt over the top and a pair of jogging bottoms. Her pink ballet shoes looked a bit floppy and worn out, and she pulled a pair of socks over the top of them. But she still looked like a dancer. I think that even if she'd put on ten jumpers and ten pairs of trousers it wouldn't have hidden the fact that she's a dancer. She already had her hair in a ponytail but she twizzled it round and jabbed in two hairgrips to keep it in place. Then she was ready.

"Right. Here we go."

And the next minute we were rushing up yet another flight of stairs. I could hear the piano music from here. It sounded tinny and echoey, just the same as when Mrs. Marsden plays. That's because there are no carpets or rugs or curtains to absorb the sound. We've learned about that in science at school.

The door to the room was open and there were a few chairs at the side. Then the rest of the room had a black floor and *barres* round all four sides, with a mirror taking up the whole of one wall. I sat down in one of the chairs, hardly daring to breathe in case I interrupted anything, while Anna went over and whispered something into the ear of an old man who was sitting in a chair with a walking stick, in front of the mirror, watching the class. He nodded, then keeping his eyes on the dancers, beckoned me to come over. Anna did a mime that I should take off my shoes, so I did that and then hurried across to his chair. When I was nearly beside him he pointed down to the floor. I sat down, feeling like a little dog obeying its master, even though I had no idea who on earth he was or what he was doing there.

When I looked round properly I got a shock because I wasn't expecting there to be male dancers all mixed in with the girls. I counted eighteen dancers altogether, and every one of them was wearing hotchpotch higgledy-piggledy clothes, like tracksuit bottoms with shorts on top of them, and all different layers on the top half. Lots of them had socks on top of their ballet shoes, and the girls had their hair tied back in ponytails, or if it was very long in a rough sort of bun. But when you watched what they were doing you didn't notice their clothes any more or their bags and water bottles tucked against the wall beside them.

The music was big and strong and the *pliés* they were doing were all mixed up in a long chain of steps with *tendus* and *port de bras*. I'd never be able to remember such a long sequence in a million years, and they danced as though they were on a stage. It was amazing and absolutely perfect. There wasn't a single thing that the teacher could possibly correct. And that thought gave me a shock. Where *was* the teacher? Maybe she'd just popped out for a moment. Or maybe she was one of the dancers on the *barre*. This wasn't like my class, where it was obvious who the teacher was. In a class of professionals, the teacher probably isn't any better than anyone else. I looked carefully at every single dancer. If one of them was in charge, they were hiding it very well. Anna was doing some stretches at the back. We all think Rose is flexible, but not compared to Anna. I couldn't believe the way she could stretch her leg up by her ear and keep it there without her hand helping at all.

"*Tendus!*" The old man's soft raspy voice suddenly filled the quiet.

I was shocked. Surely he wasn't allowed to interrupt the class like that? But a second later I realized something massive, and I think my mouth was probably hanging open when I looked at him the next time. The old man *was* the ballet teacher! He got to his feet, went to the middle of the room, dropped his cane and began to half demonstrate, half explain the next sequence, in a mixture of English with French for the ballet terms. It was just as though someone had tipped magic dust over him and turned him into a brilliant dancer. He was balancing and turning out perfectly. The exercise was really complicated again, but the dancers looked as though they understood. Then the pianist played an introduction, the dancers began and the old man went to sit down again. But he saw that he'd left his cane in the middle of the room, and made a tutting noise as though he was cross with himself. In a flash I jumped up, got the cane and handed it to him.

"Thank you, young lady." But he was concentrating on watching the dancers.

As the *barre* work carried on, my body kept nearly joining in by mistake. It's so hard sitting completely still when every single part of you tingles to dance. Right in the middle of a complicated exercise with *ronds de jambe* the old man flapped his hand at the pianist and he immediately stopped playing. The dancers came a bit away from the *barre* and watched the teacher carefully. He was facing the big mirror.

"You see, it's a line…" he said in a quiet voice. "And the line starts here…" His arm was in front of him, but he gently took it round to the side as his head came up and his eyes followed his hand. "D'you see the follow-through there?"

The dancers were all trying it out, and I watched them and thought they really did look much better than they had done before. I think that was the moment when I realized this old man was a brilliant teacher even if he couldn't dance like he probably had done when he was younger.

"Yes, *that's* right! *You've* got it!"

I looked round to see who he was talking to, and got the shock of my life because he was looking at me. Without even realizing it, I'd been trying it out too, lifting my arm in front of me and taking it to the side without breaking the line.

"Up you get, young lady. Let's try that again."

I felt terrible because I was interrupting the class and I was sure everyone really wanted to get on, but I didn't dare stay sitting down when I'd been told to get up. So I quickly stood in first position, feeling a bit funny wearing just my socks, and tried to find Anna's eyes in the mirror. They were smiling encouragingly at me, which made me feel better. The old man nodded at me, which I think meant that I was supposed to do the arm movement again, so I did. When I'd done it he just kept staring at my arm and I wasn't sure if I was supposed to do it again. But that might have made him cross, so I just stayed in the position with my arm to the side and eventually he nodded and said, "Good. That's the idea."

Then he turned to the class. "*Frappés!*" And a few seconds later the class were doing the fastest beating-feet exercise I'd ever seen.

I sat back down on the floor without a sound and hugged my knees tight. I know I'd only done one little arm movement but I *could* actually now say that I'd joined in a proper, professional class with Anna Lane. I felt like dancing round the room and shouting it out loud but of course I couldn't do *that*, so I hugged the excitement even tighter and carried on watching.

5 The Best Time

The class got better and better. After the *barre*, a few dancers took off their sweatshirts and some of them rolled their jogging bottoms up. It looked quite funny, especially the ones who'd only rolled up one leg, but no one even looked at anyone else, so they must have been completely used to each other's strange clothes. Every face was glowing with sweat because they'd all been working so hard, and I noticed the sweat was starting to come through their tops too. Anna had rolled up her jogging bottoms and peeled off her sweatshirt.

I thought she looked brilliant with her muscles all tight and strong.

The dancers didn't go in rows, they just stood in spaces. The centre work was even more amazing than the *barre*. They all raised their legs so high and no one wobbled on their supporting leg even though they had to stay balanced on one leg for about twenty seconds, while their arms and the other leg moved.

The steps that the teacher set them seemed to get faster and faster and more and more complicated. Anna twizzled and leaped and stretched and shone like the biggest star, and it was so inspirational I had tears in my eyes. When it came to an exercise with *pirouettes*, which are when you spin round, everyone could do triples easily and one of the men even did a sixer! I couldn't wait to tell Rose about that. She loves *pirouettes*. The dancers seemed to work harder and harder, even though I didn't think that was possible. And when they started doing jumps I saw that their tops were absolutely drenched with sweat.

At Miss Coralie's, I'm usually quite good at remembering sequences, but here it was impossible. I was determined to keep trying though. So I marked everything the old man said with my hands, because it was obvious everyone had completely forgotten about me by then.

"Want to join in?" My heart nearly stopped beating because the old man must have spotted my dancing hands and he was looking down at me.

"Erm...I haven't got my ballet shoes with me."

"No need for ballet shoes, so long as you've got your feet with you!"

There was a little ripple of laughter and I realized the dancers liked the old man even though he was quite scary.

"I'm not sure if I'm good enough..."

"Nonsense. Do what you can."

Anna gave me a twinkly look and one of her biggest smiles where her dimples show, and it felt as though we were best friends getting excited because I'd been invited to her house for tea. Everyone started doing stretching exercises and the old man looked at the ceiling as he marked something with his hands and hummed loudly. He seemed to have gone into his own little world. I think he was giving me the chance to take my place. I went right to the very back, and a big surge of nervousness made my mouth go dry. I took my jumper off and put it neatly at the side. Now I'd just got a thin top on like everyone else.

"Get yourself warmed up at the *barre*, young lady."

I hoped he'd carry straight on because I didn't want anyone to watch me doing *pliés* or anything. My hand holding the *barre* was shaking a bit and my knees felt like jelly.

But a few seconds later everyone was dancing the next sequence and no one was looking at me. I managed to make my grade five *plié* exercise fit the music by doing some bits quicker and some slower. It was good fun doing it to different music. When I'd done it on both sides, I went on to *battements glissés* and then did some *grands battements* and some stretches with my foot on the *barre*. I knew I was warmed up and ready to join in, but I didn't dare. Everyone would stare and I'd feel clumsy and stupid. Maybe I'd just do one more thing at the *barre*. So I tried the *ronds de jambe en l'air* and the music fitted perfectly. But that's when I started to realize something. No one was dancing any more. I looked round and got a big shock. Everyone was watching me. Anna was smiling and nodding, trying to make me feel comfortable, but inside I was squirming with embarrassment. I stopped straight away.

"Brava!" said the old man. "Bravissima! What is your name?"

"Jasmine Ayed," I answered quietly, feeling the biggest spurt of happiness that I think I've ever felt go whizzing round my body. The old man liked my dancing. He'd even stopped to watch me. I expect he was just being kind, but it was still a brilliant feeling.

"Hmm…" He seemed to be studying my face. I stayed perfectly still until he suddenly nodded again and said, "Right, find a place, Jasmine."

I stayed at the back and he went straight on with the next sequence, and from that moment on, no one watched me again. They just let me blend in, so every time I felt stupid for getting it completely wrong or not being able to keep up, it didn't seem to matter.

By the end of the lesson I'd learned so much and felt so happy. I'd always known for certain that I wanted to make ballet my career, but now I knew for triple positive. And at that moment I had a big surge of ambition to pass the audition for the Junior Associates. It would be so completely wonderful.

I managed to pluck up enough courage to thank the teacher, and he shook my hand and said, "Well done, Jasmine." I felt sort of special because he didn't let go of my hand straight away, but kept looking into my eyes as if he was searching for something, then said, "Hmm. Well done."

"Did you enjoy yourself?" Anna asked me as we went outside to wait for Papa.

"I think it was the best thing I've ever done in my life," I told her truthfully.

"Really! That's fantastic! I'm so pleased I invited you."

"I'll treasure these cards for ever," I said, looking at the four beautiful ballet photos I'd picked up from reception. "Thank you for autographing them."

"That's all right. Actually, maybe you should have got Maurice to sign them.

"Maurice?"

"Maurice Chase, the teacher. He was a fantastic dancer in his day, then he turned to choreography when he retired. He choreographed two of the new dances for our tour. We'll be rehearsing them in a few minutes."

"Oh, wow! When did he retire?"

"Years ago. We dancers don't usually go on past our thirties, you know."

"Margot Fonteyn was in her fifties though, wasn't she?"

"You *do* know your stuff, don't you?" Anna said, with a smile.

"I've got a beautiful book at home called *The Art of Margot Fonteyn*."

I was just about to ask her who her all-time favourite dancer was, when the door opened behind us and out came Maurice Chase.

"One o'clock start, Anna. All right?"

She nodded and he turned to go off down the road at exactly the same moment as Anna nudged my arm. "Look! There's someone waving over there. Is that your dad?"

I followed her eyes and saw that Papa's car had pulled up. He was beckoning me out of the window.

"Yes, that's him. I'll have to go. Thank you very very much, Anna, for the best day of my life."

She kissed me and gave me a hug. "You're a darling. I'll see you next time I'm down at Mum's."

A wave of sadness came over me because soon I'd have nothing but four photos as a souvenir of this magical day, and before I could stop myself I asked Anna if I could possibly have her phone number.

"Course you can." But straight away we both realized that neither of us had anything to write with. "Hang on, I'll rush back into reception…"

But I could see that Papa was getting a bit impatient, beckoning to me to hurry up. "Just tell me…I'll remember it and write it down as soon as I get in the car."

"Okay, I'll tell you my home number because it's easier to remember than my mobile."

I already knew that London numbers start with 020, so then there were only eight more numbers to remember and they weren't very difficult.

"Thank you again!"

She laughed. "Go on! I'll speak to you soon."

Papa gave Anna a wave and a smile as I ran to the car. "Hello, Jasmine. You look happy. Had a good time?"

"The best!" I said in a bit of a dreamy voice because I was concentrating on Anna's number.

"Excellent. It's a good thing to have different experiences in life, isn't it?"

I nodded happily. It was great that Papa seemed to be properly interested, even though he's not exactly the world's biggest ballet fan. As soon as I got into the car, I wrote down Anna's number on the back of one of my Rambert cards, then started gabbling on about the class.

"The ballet teacher was quite old but still a brilliant teacher, *and* he's a famous choreographer. I mean *really* famous. His name's Maurice Chase. He's choreographed two of the new dances for the Rambert tour."

"Uh-huh..."

I knew Papa was probably concentrating on driving, because there was a lot of traffic about, but he didn't seem so interested any more. I'd thought he would have been impressed about me meeting a famous choreographer. Wait till he heard about me joining in with the class, though. That would surprise him. I specially waited till we'd reached a quieter bit of road so that he could concentrate fully.

"He was quite scary and strict...the ballet teacher..."

"Yes, what did you say his name was?"

"Maurice Chase."

"Hmmm." Papa was frowning, but at least he was taking a bit more interest now, so I carried on.

"And guess what, he let me join in!"

"Lucky girl!"

I'd been watching Papa's face. He looked very tired, but he also looked thoughtful, frowning at the road with his eyebrows almost touching each other. It was quite a scary sight.

"Hmmmm, yes..."

My whole body felt suddenly tired, so I flopped back in my seat and closed my eyes. Part of me was dying to talk and talk about every little detail of the lesson, but my feelings were too big and special to tell someone who wasn't as excited as me about it. I decided to wait till I got home, then phone Poppy and Rose straight away. The next day I could tell them even more and show them the steps I'd danced for Maurice Chase. We could have a whole ballet day. Yessss!

6 The Sad Look

"Are you going to tell Miss Coralie?"

"I don't know. I hadn't even thought about that."

Poppy, Rose and I were in my room, sitting cross-legged on the floor. We'd been talking about Anna's class for the last half hour.

"You ought to tell her," said Poppy. "It's important news, you know."

"But when? We have to be silent when we come in and then we get straight on with the class and then we go out silently."

"You'll just have to break the silence,"

said Rose. "It's perfectly easy. You just say, 'Excuse me, Miss Coralie, but have *you* ever been taught by Maurice Catch?'"

"*Chase!*" Poppy and I corrected Rose, through our laughing.

We spent the rest of the morning and half the afternoon choreographing our own special ballet. We called it "Souvenir" and it was supposed to stand for the lovely memory of Anna's class.

After Poppy and Rose had gone, Maman and I went to see Miss Bird.

"So, did you have a wonderful time, my dear?"

I knew exactly what she was talking about. "Oh yes, it was absolutely brilliant, Miss Bird."

She leaned forwards. "Anna tells me it was old Maurice Chase taking the class."

I nodded. "He let me join in."

"So I gather. I bet you were in seventh heaven, weren't you?"

I nodded even harder.

"Good girl! And now you can say that

you've danced with the stars!"

When it was time for us to go, Miss Bird told Maman that she wouldn't see her at the next committee meeting because she'd been invited to stay with her sister at the seaside for a couple of weeks.

"The sea air will do you good," Maman said. "At least that's what my mother says!"

And as the two of them carried on talking, I was thinking about next term. In one way, I was desperate for term to start so the audition would be nearer and also because I was dying to tell Miss Coralie about Anna's class. But I still felt anxious when I thought what Papa might say about the audition.

On the first Tuesday of term, I was so excited. I'd decided to talk to Miss Coralie about Anna's class at the end of the lesson when everyone had gone. But when we were in the changing room getting ready, Poppy suddenly surprised me.

"Guess what, everyone? Jazz met Anna Lane, the famous dancer, over the holidays, and Anna invited her to go to one of her classes in London!"

"A class with proper professional dancers!" said Immy. "Wow!"

"That's incredible!" said Lottie.

"You're so lucky!" said Sophie. "Was it really cool?"

I nodded happily because I'd been a bit worried about seeming like a show-off, but everyone was smiling and crowding round me. Well, everyone except Tamsyn.

"*And...*" said Poppy, "Jazz was allowed to join in!"

There were loads of gasps. "Join *in*! With the actual class? Whoa! That's so brill!"

"Who was the teacher?" asked Tamsyn calmly, with her eyes on her ballet shoes as she tucked the drawstrings in. She was pretending that it was nothing special joining in a class with professionals. Tamsyn doesn't like it when she's not the most important one. It's true that she's really good at ballet, but it's also true that she knows it. I still didn't want to sound showy-offy though.

"It was a man called Maurice Chase. He's a choreographer too." I deliberately did a giggle. "He's very old and at first I thought he was just someone sitting at the front, but then he started telling everyone what to do."

Quite a few girls joined in my giggle, including Poppy, even though she'd heard me tell the story over and over.

"I've never heard of Maurice Chase. Have you, Immy?" said Tamsyn, sitting up straight with her feet touching each other and her knees flat on the ground. (She's easily the most supple girl in the class.)

"Don't ask me. I've never heard of *any* choreographers," said Immy.

"You can't demonstrate properly if you're

old, can you?" Tamsyn went on, opening her legs out into a V-shape and putting her top half flat on the floor.

"It seems a bit weird," said Lottie.

"No, he was really good, honestly—" I started to say.

But Tamsyn interrupted. "Hey, can anyone do this?" Then she raised her legs and leaned back a bit, so she was balancing on her bottom with her top and bottom halves making a V in the air.

Everyone except me and Poppy got down on the floor to try it.

"She's only jealous," whispered Poppy, tucking her arm through mine, as we went out into the corridor. It was nearly time for Rose's class to finish and ours to start. "I hope she hears you telling Miss Coralie about it, because I bet Miss Coralie's heard of Maurice Chase, and then Tamsyn'll realize that he *is* famous."

"It wouldn't make any difference," I told

Poppy. "She just doesn't like it that I've done something she hasn't."

"You're so sensible and grown up, Jasmine," said Poppy. "I wish I could be like you."

I was just about to tell her that she'd hate to be me with all my school work and piano practice and everything, when the changing-room door opened behind us and everyone got into a silent line. A second later the door to the room where we do class opened and out came the grade fours. Rose was right at the back. She gave me and Poppy a cross-eyed look with her tongue hanging out, and her shoulders drooping, which is her way of showing us that she's exhausted. We both stifled our giggles then ran in on tiptoes to take our places at the *barre*.

I was right at the front and when I looked at Miss Coralie I saw that she was already looking at me. Only there was something wrong with her look. It was sort of sad.

A moment later everyone was ready to start and Miss Coralie was smiling round the whole class. "Welcome back, girls. Get ready for *pliés*. Preparation...and..."

Then it was just as though the whole Easter holidays had never even happened because everything was straight back to normal. It felt lovely doing a proper class after three weeks of practising in my room.

When we were doing the *barre* work, I tried to make my arm do the line that Mr. Chase had talked about, and twice Miss Coralie said, "Nice, Jasmine." The second time my head was tipped sideways and I couldn't help flicking my eyes a tiny bit to look at Miss Coralie. It gave me a little jolt because she was wearing the same sad look that she'd been wearing at the beginning of class. I wished I could ask her what the matter was, but of course I couldn't.

As the class went on, I thought about Anna's

class quite a few times. I'm sure it made me dance better than usual because Miss Coralie said, "Lovely, Jasmine," when we were doing a step sequence with *pas de bourrées*.

At the end of the class when we'd done the *révérence*, Poppy mouthed "Go on!" to me. I waited till I was the only one left, then went to the front.

"Can I tell you my exciting news?" I said to Miss Coralie.

Her face lit up straight away as though she was absolutely dying to hear my news. And even Mrs. Marsden stopped what she was doing to listen.

"I went to a proper professional class with Anna Lune, Miss Bird's daughter, in the holidays..."

"Oh!"

It was funny because a little bit of the light seemed to have gone out of her face. Unless I just imagined that.

"And I was allowed to join in!"

"Oh, how absolutely wonderful, Jasmine! What a marvellous experience." The light came back then. "Tell me all about it."

I'd never realized what a gentle, understanding person Miss Coralie is. She didn't seem half as strict as usual. It was as easy as anything talking to her. She asked all the questions I wanted her to ask and by the time I'd finished talking to her I really felt as though I'd had the whole brilliant experience all over again.

But when I was at the door, just about to go out, I turned round and got a shock of my own because Miss Coralie and Mrs. Marsden were looking at each other, and they were both wearing really sad looks. This time I definitely wasn't imagining it.

Definitely.

7 Planning What to Do

I couldn't get that look of Miss Coralie's out of my head and I was desperate to talk to Poppy and Rose about it. I asked Maman if they could come over after school the next day and she agreed, which was really incredible. I'm not usually allowed friends round during the week, you see.

So on Wednesday after school we went straight up to my room.

"It's great that your mum let us come round on a school day, isn't it?" said Poppy.

I nodded quickly. "I wanted to ask you something."

They both leaned forwards. "What?"

"Did you think Miss Coralie looked at me in a...funny way, Poppy?"

Poppy seemed to hesitate. "I'm not sure."

"Well, I noticed quite a few times. Even after I'd told her about Anna's class. But...I don't get why."

"Aha! You need Detective Rose Bedford on the case! Now, Miss Ayed, please describe this look precisely."

I didn't want Rose treating it as a joke. It might be nothing terrible, but something wasn't quite right. I was certain of that.

"She just looked sad."

Rose stopped playing detective and frowned. "And she didn't give anyone else the same sad look?"

I shook my head. "I don't think so."

"Right, this is what you do," said Rose. "You wait until next Tuesday, then you notice whether Miss Coralie does it again, and if she does, you go up to her at the end and you say, "Excuse me, Miss Coralie, but why do you keep looking at me as though I've got something the matter with me?"

"Yes, it's like she thinks there's something the matter with me...it's exactly that."

Rose looked alarmed. "But there isn't anything the matter with you, is there?"

"No, course not – and anyway, why would Miss Coralie know about it, if I didn't even know myself?"

It went silent after that and I suddenly realized that Poppy wasn't really joining in this conversation and, what's more, she'd gone very pink.

Rose must have noticed too. "What do *you* think, Poppy?"

"I don't know," said Poppy, looking down.

"I said, 'What do you *think*?'" Rose said, leaning forwards.

So then Poppy had to say something. "It's

probably stupid..." she said slowly, "but...do you think she might have...phoned your parents, Jasmine, and said something to them about how she wants you to audition for the Junior Associates?"

"But Miss Coralie hasn't even told *me* the date yet," I said.

I wanted to swallow, but my mouth seemed too dry because I'd suddenly had a picture of the time I'd blurted out to Anna about the auditions in the supermarket car park. And then I'd purposely told Maman that I didn't want Papa to know until we knew the date. But she must have gone ahead and told him anyway.

"Maman's told him," I said in a whisper. "That's it! That's what's happened!" The tears were gathering like little pinpricks at the corners of my eyes. "And Papa must have phoned Miss Coralie and told her I'm not allowed." My voice was getting louder because

I was getting crosser. "And that explains why Maman let you two come round even though it's the middle of the week. She's being nice to me, to make up for being horrible in another way."

The three of us looked at one another and then I shot out of the room like an arrow and I knew they were following. We raced downstairs and ran into the kitchen.

"Did you tell Papa that Miss Coralie wants me to audition for the Junior Associates?" I said fiercely.

Maman was running the water at the sink and she turned the tap off, but didn't turn round straight away. I knew then, and I couldn't help shouting. "You *did,* didn't you? And then I suppose he phoned Miss Coralie and said I wasn't allowed."

When Maman looked at me her face was pale, and when she spoke, her voice was shaky. "Yes...he did. But Jasmeen it would have made no difference whether I'd told Papa first or Miss Coralie had spoken to him. You know you can't give up all your Saturdays, don't you?"

I heard Poppy gasp behind me. Then Rose strode forwards and put her arm round my shoulder. A second later, Poppy was on the other side of me and there we stood, facing Maman.

"Why can't I just audition? It's not fair!" I screeched out like a little girl. Then I burst into tears and Rose and Poppy were both hugging me.

"I know it's a tough thing for you to accept, *chérie*," said Maman, turning suddenly brisk, "but you've still got your lessons with Miss Coralie, haven't you?" She started wiping the kitchen table, even though it was totally clean. "Your father did actually ask Miss Coralie not to say anything..."

"She didn't!" I shouted. "She just looked

sad. Because she *is* sad. You're the cruellest parents in the whole world!"

All the time I was shouting at Maman, I knew I should really be shouting at Papa. He was the one who had made the decision, just like it was him who had tried to make me give up ballet before.

"I know you can't see it at the moment, Jasmeen, but your father is only doing what's best for you. You're getting on so well at school and your teacher thinks you could become a doctor if you carry on as you are now, but that's not going to happen unless you have enough time to study."

"I don't want to be a doctor. I want to be a ballerina!" I shouted back.

"When you're older you'll thank Papa, you know, because very few dancers ever get the chance of success, and all the others stay in the *corps de ballet*, earning a pittance and then retire in their twenties or thirties.

What kind of a life is that?"

"The life I want."

"Well, I'm not arguing with you any more. You can talk to your father when he comes back tomorrow evening."

"No, I'm not talking to him ever again!" I shouted, then I banged out of the room, with Poppy and Rose just behind me again, and we raced upstairs and back into my room.

"Don't start crying!" said Rose in an urgent voice that made me stop in my tracks.

"Why?"

"Because we need to work out a plan. And if you're crying we won't be able to."

"I've told you my plan. I'm never speaking to him again!"

I sat down heavily on my bed, and then slid onto the floor.

"You've got to talk to your dad sometime, Jasmine," Poppy said softly.

I drew my knees up tight, resting my cheek

on them, my face turned away from Poppy and Rose because more tears were beginning to fall now. "There's nothing I can say."

Poppy sat down beside me and Rose crouched in front of me.

"You mustn't give up, Jasmine," said Poppy. "Rose and I will think of a plan, honestly."

Then Rose suddenly jumped up. "Yes! Come on! Thumb-thumb!"

She sounded all bright and cheery but I could tell she wasn't feeling at all cheerful really, because she knew as well as I did that it was hopeless trying to think of things to say to make Papa change his mind.

We did the thumb-thumb though, once Poppy and Rose had managed to drag me up from the floor. Then Rose suddenly announced that there *was* a solution.

"Only one person can help you, Jazz," she said, looking me straight in the eyes, "and that's Miss Coralie. So listen carefully..."

8 The End of the Matter

The next day was Thursday and Papa didn't get home till late, thank goodness, so I just said, "I'm going to bed now." Then I walked out of the room without even saying, "Night."

On Friday when I got home from school, Papa said, "Hello Jasmine," in his brightest voice and gave me an extra-big smile.

I said a really quick hello and then right away started flicking through a magazine that was on the kitchen table, because I wanted to be as horrible as possible without him saying that I was being cheeky.

After a moment he looked a bit cross and sat down opposite me, and that's when he started to talk about what had happened.

"Look, I know you're upset, but as Maman's told you, I can't have you using up every Saturday with extra ballet. If you take the journey to London and back, and then the time it'll take to get to Covent Garden, plus the two hours for the class, that's practically the whole day. I don't think you realize how much more work you're going to get when you're at your new school. And if you don't do the work then you won't get the results. And these days, it's harder and harder to get into a good university…"

I completely forgot about never speaking to him again. I jumped out of my chair and glared at him as hard as I dared.

"I don't want to go to university! I want to be a ballerina. You think I'm really good at it. You said so after the show."

"Yes, you *are* really good at ballet, Jasmine. You're also really good at a lot of things, but ballet is something that you'll grow out of. Lots of little girls have got ballerina dreams or they want to be pop idols or famous actresses. And how many of them ever make it? Very, very few!"

"I'm not going to grow out of it *ever!*" I shouted.

"Look, Jasmine, you can be as mad as you like for as long as you like, but it won't make any difference to my decision. Extra ballet in any shape or form is not something that you will be doing, so you might as well forget about it. You can go on with your weekly lessons with Miss Coralie, but ballet is not the career for you, and that's the end of the matter."

My eyes were swimming with tears and I didn't know what to do.

Papa's voice softened a bit. "Tell me about your day."

I shrugged and kept my eyes on the magazine. "Okay." I spoke quickly in my most bored voice. "Assembly, work, break, work, lunch, work, the end."

The moment I'd finished I felt my cheeks getting hot. Papa was going to explode now.

But he just walked out of the kitchen, and Maman threw me a big frown as she followed him. I sat down at the table and flopped forwards with my head resting on my arms and my eyes filling with tears.

I couldn't wait for ballet on Tuesday. I kept hearing Poppy's voice telling me I mustn't give up, no matter how sad I felt, and Rose insisting that I talked to Miss Coralie. And it was true that Miss Coralie *was* my only hope now. I just prayed that she'd help me change Papa's mind.

9 Not Over Yet

When Tuesday finally came I went into class
with my heart beating like mad, but then
incredibly I actually forgot about Papa during
the lesson because there were just too many
ballet things to think about to leave room for
any other thoughts. The only time my body
did a little shiver of fear was when I saw that
same sad look in Miss Coralie's eyes and I
remembered that I was going to talk to her at
the end.

She must have been expecting me to speak,
because as soon as we'd done the *révérence* she

was looking at me again. I waited till there was just me and Poppy left in the room, then together we walked to the front. I kept my eyes on the ground. It would be easier like that. Rose's words were all ready in my head and I got them out quickly before I could change my mind.

"I know my dad has told you that I'm not allowed to audition for Junior Associates, and I can't make him change his mind on my own, so I was wondering if you could talk to him again."

I raised my eyes then, because the speech was finished but Miss Coralie wasn't saying anything. She looked at me for ages and all sorts of horrible thoughts went whizzing through my mind.

"I mean...only if you still want me to audition."

She started to talk quickly then. "Of course I want you to. It's what I did myself when I was young, and it led me straight to *corps de ballet* at the Royal Ballet company, before I became a soloist. And in some ways you remind me of myself, Jasmine."

My body swayed with happiness. That was such a compliment.

"Oh, *please*, Miss Coralie. Could you phone Papa and see if you can make him change his mind?"

The sad look was back on Miss Coralie's face.

"Jasmine, I'm so sorry… I've already told your parents how talented you are, but your father is adamant that you're not to do the audition, so I'm afraid there's nothing else I can do. Maybe he'll change his mind next year…"

I looked at her and knew straight away that she didn't really believe that would happen.

I nodded because I couldn't speak. Then Poppy and I turned and walked to the door.

It seemed such a long way in the silence that I felt as though someone had died.

Rose phoned me that evening to find out what Miss Coralie had said.

"She can't do anything," I explained heavily. "She just said that maybe he'd let me audition next year."

Rose started gabbling. "Don't worry, because I've got another plan – a much better one. You ought to talk to Anna."

"Anna! What can *she* do?"

"She can explain to your dad that he doesn't realize how good you are and that the sooner you get started with Saturday lessons, the bigger your chances of making it to the top would be. Because that's what he wants, isn't it? He wants you to be successful."

"The trouble is, he wants me to be successful at medicine or law or something to do with money, or banks or...just anything but ballet."

"Yes, but that might be because he still doesn't realize how good you are, even though Miss Coralie says so. Anna's a professional dancer. She'll be able to tell him because she's seen you with her own eyes!"

"But what if I'm *not* good enough, Rose? I can't phone Anna up and say, 'Oh please tell my dad that I'm good enough to be a soloist.' She'd probably just laugh and tell me not to be silly."

"At least if you phone and ask, you'll have given yourself a chance, won't you?"

After I'd put the phone down, I sat staring at the carpet for ages, thinking about what Rose had said. Then I picked the phone up again and tapped in Poppy's number. She listened carefully when I told her Rose's idea.

"Rose is right, Jasmine. You've got to phone Anna. Just talk to her about how upset you are and maybe she'll offer to have a word with your dad, without you having to ask her yourself."

So this time when I put the phone down I felt better. I could just talk to Anna about everything and wait and see what she said. Right, I'd do it straight away before I could change my mind.

There were eight rings, then an answer-phone message. I took a deep breath and left my message in a bit of a trembly voice. I wasn't deliberately making it tremble, it was just doing it on its own.

"Hello, Anna. It's Jasmine. I don't know what to do because Papa has told Miss Coralie that I'm not allowed to do the audition for Junior Associates, and he won't change his mind whatever Miss Coralie says. So I...thought I'd phone you...to see if you can think of anything...I can do. Um...thank you very much." Then I left my number and rang off.

After that I started staring at the carpet again, as though the phone was more likely to ring if I kept completely still and was all ready for it. It never did, though, and I know it sounds dramatic but I sunk deeper and deeper into despair as the evening went on.

The next day at school was even worse. I had to read out loud in front of the class. I got my words mixed up and didn't do very well but I didn't mind at all, because reading out loud is nothing compared to ballet. I couldn't wait for Maman to pick me up at the end of school.

"Did Anna phone?" I said the moment I got in the car.

"Anna? No."

My heart felt like a hard pebble, falling down through my body. I'd been so sure she would have phoned. Papa was due back at eight o'clock and I was really praying that Anna would phone before he got home.

Not Over Yet

At seven o'clock I couldn't bear it any longer and decided to phone her again.

Please answer, Anna. Please answer.

But it was only the answerphone message, and that's when it suddenly hit me. Of course! Anna had said she was going on tour. At first I felt like crying. If only I'd taken her mobile phone number instead of her home one. But wait a minute...I could get her mobile number from her mum, couldn't I? I found Miss Bird's number easily enough in Maman's phone book, and then had to put up with listening to another horrible load of rings before I remembered that Miss Bird had said she was going to stay with her sister at the seaside. So then I felt like crying again. This whole thing was turning into the most terrible nightmare. What was I going to do now? I was completely out of ideas.

10 The Package

That week was one of the worst of my life. The only good thing about it was that I didn't have to see Papa because he was away for most of it. Poppy and Rose couldn't even cheer me up on Saturday, and by Monday I didn't think it was possible to be any more miserable.

After school I was helping Maman in the kitchen when I heard the dreaded sound of Papa's key in the door. He was much earlier than usual. It was only quarter to five. I carried on putting the dishes away without even looking up when he came into the kitchen. He kissed Maman then said hello to me and sat down at the kitchen table.

"I've got something for you, Jasmine."

I turned round and saw that he'd put an envelope on the table. On the front of it was written *Doctor Ayed.* Papa took out another envelope from inside and handed it to me. It said *Jasmine Ayed* in the same handwriting. I looked at Maman.

She seemed as surprised as me. "Open it, then, Jasmeen."

Inside was a glossy photograph and a letter on very thin paper. The photo was of a male dancer in the middle of a high leap with his arms and head flung back. I had to stare at the signature for ages before I realized what it said *Maurice Chase.*

I gasped and felt my cheeks flooding with colour. "It's a photo of Anna's teacher, Maman. Look! That's what he looked like before he got old."

"Read the letter," said Papa.

I looked at him to try and find out what was happening. I didn't understand what was going on or how Papa had got this letter. But his face just looked tired. I began to read out loud...

Dear Jasmine,

Anna asked me to send you the enclosed photo of myself in my dancing days. She said that you were surprised to find such an elderly ballet teacher! I'm afraid that's what comes of having taken the route expected of me by my family, before returning to where my heart lay and taking up ballet seriously. I was older than most when I became a solo dancer, and older still when I moved into choreography.

Good luck in the future, Jasmine. Continue to work hard and I'm sure the world of ballet

will be seeing a great deal more of you.
With my very best wishes,
Maurice Chase

For ages after I'd read the last words, I couldn't stop staring at the letter. To think I was actually holding a letter written specially to me from such a famous dancer. It was my most precious possession and I knew I'd keep it for ever. But then I suddenly came back to earth with a bang when I realized that whatever Mr. Chase said, there was no way I was ever going to be a professional dancer. I couldn't help the tears that came into my eyes.

Papa was taking another letter out of the envelope that was addressed to him.

"How did you get hold of the package, *chéri?*" Maman asked him, frowning at the envelope.

"It came to the hospital. Maurice dropped it off by hand."

There was something not quite right about what Papa had just said and I couldn't think what it was. Still...I started to go because I wanted to find a special place in my room for my photo and an even more special place for my letter.

"Don't you want to hear what Maurice has written in his letter to me?" asked Papa.

And suddenly I realized what it was that was odd. Papa was saying his name as though he actually knew Maurice Chase.

I stopped with my hand on the door handle and stood still as Papa started to read, but it was only a few seconds before I turned round and leaned against the door, feeling weak at the knees.

Dear Dr. Ayed,

Please forgive my using this "hospital route" to convey the enclosed photograph to Jasmine.

I'm afraid I failed to note down her address but was particularly keen to make sure she received the photo, as her presence in my class made such a tremendous impact on all of us here.

I thought I recognized Jasmine as soon as I saw her and when she told me her name I knew there could be no doubt that she was your daughter. I was a heart patient of yours some years ago. I don't know if you remember me, but I shall always remember you. You must be very proud to have a daughter with such talent and determination to succeed in such a very difficult field.

Yours most sincerely,

Maurice Chase

Papa kept the letter in his hand but dropped his hand to the table.

"And *do* you remember Mr. Chase being your patient?" Maman asked.

Papa nodded. "Very well. We struck up quite a friendship over the weeks that he was in my care. But, sadly, we lost touch with each other, and I hadn't heard from him for years until I got this letter."

Papa looked as though saying those words had made him exhausted. I didn't want to stop this conversation though. There were so many questions I wanted to ask.

"Why did he say that he'd always remember you, Papa?"

There was a pause, then Papa spoke quickly and quietly as though he wanted to throw the words away. "I saved his life."

I couldn't help gasping, but I didn't speak because the words seemed too big for anything to come after them.

In the end it was Papa who broke the silence himself. "I got the letter at lunchtime and decided to go along to the Rambert Studios to see if Maurice was there. He was, and we managed to snatch a quick lunch together."

"Lunch! With Maurice Chase! You're so lucky!" The words just popped out.

Maman smiled and reached out for Papa's hand. "That must have been wonderful, *chéri*."

There was a short silence, then Papa spoke very quietly. "I've never known anyone fight death with such determination as that man did. At the time, I always wondered where he found the strength, and today he explained it. He said that as a dancer you not only have to have great physical strength, but even greater mental strength. I'd never thought about that before and we talked about it for some time." Papa turned to Maman. "So, yes, *chérie*, it was a wonderful lunch. Wonderfully interesting! And far too short, but we both had to get back to work."

My eyes went back to my precious letter and it was completely silent in the kitchen as I read the words to myself once more.

"Maurice was telling me at lunch how his parents insisted that he went to university to study law," said Papa slowly.

"But he came back to ballet when he was old enough to do what he wanted," I said in hardly more than a whisper.

"Yes... And I wonder," Papa went on, "whether his parents would have continued to pressurize him into following that other route, if they'd had any idea at all that he'd have the determination and fight in him to go straight back to what he really wanted to do, the moment he was able to."

I couldn't believe that this was Papa talking. His voice wasn't strong. And he looked all bewildered and exhausted. I'd never ever seen him like this. Maman was stroking his hand, and it suddenly felt as though Papa wasn't so in charge any more. I didn't know what to say, so I just mumbled something about going to my room to make a frame for my photo.

It was a funny evening. Papa and Maman stayed in the kitchen most of the time. I did my piano practice, then I was allowed to eat tea in front of the television. After that, I did my homework in my room with my favourite ballet CD playing in the background. When I went to bed I still felt strange. It was as though I was holding my breath, but I didn't know why.

11 Maurice's Magic

At breakfast the next morning, it was just Maman and me because Papa had already left early for work.

"I'm going to phone Poppy's and Rose's mums this morning," Maman suddenly said when I was pouring out my cereal.

I looked up because there was something mysterious about her voice. "Why?"

"To see if the girls can join us at the Chinese restaurant tonight."

"We're going out for a meal tonight? Why?"

"It was Papa's idea. He thought it would be nice to celebrate."

By this time, Maman had a great big smile on her face and my heart was starting to race.

I spoke slowly, my eyes boring into Maman's. "To celebrate...what?"

"Papa and I talked and talked last night. You remember what he said about Maurice Chase's fight and determination? Well, now, Papa realizes that *you* have that same strength of character, and no matter how much we try to push you away from ballet, you will always go back to it in the end. That's why we made a big decision last night. So after you'd gone to bed, Papa phoned Miss Coralie to say that he is happy for you to do the audition for Saturday Royal Ballet classes."

Cornflakes and milk were spilling over my bowl on to the table because I'd forgotten to stop pouring I was in such a state of shock. Maman was laughing as I dropped the packet, leaped out of my chair and went to give her the tightest hug.

"I'm the happiest girl in the whole world," I told her. "I must tell Poppy and Rose. Can I phone them now?"

Maman was still laughing. "Go on then. And ask them about this evening. They could come over straight after ballet."

"It's going to be the best celebration ever," said Rose, as Maman turned the car into our road.

All the way home from ballet we'd been talking and talking about how brilliantly everything had turned out and how happy Miss Coralie had been. But I'd been dying to get home because I wanted to see my dad. Then I spotted his car and my heart began to race.

Maman pulled into our drive and the very second she switched off the ignition, I leaped out of the car and ran into our house through the back door. I rushed through the kitchen and the hall and up the stairs. Papa was just coming out of his and Maman's bedroom. He'd changed out of his work clothes and his face looked much younger than it had the night before.

"Oh, thank you, thank you, thank you," I said, flinging my arms round his waist and laying my head against his chest.

"It's old Maurice you've got to thank!" Papa laughed, holding me tight. Then he kissed the top of my head. "Come on, let's celebrate!"

Maman, Rose and Poppy were just coming in through the front door.

"You look nice, Doctor Ayed!" Rose called upstairs, in her usual Rose way, while Poppy went a bit pink.

"Thank you, Miss Bedford," said Papa, smiling. "I'm all set to drink a toast to Maurice."

"Right, I'll just set the answerphone, then I'm ready," said Maman, hurrying off to the kitchen.

"Have you got your letter from Maurice?" Poppy asked me a bit shyly.

"Yes, read it out, Jazz," said Rose.

So I pulled it out of my pocket.

"Hmm," said Papa as Maman came back. "It's interesting that he thinks you've got the determination to succeed, Jasmine. Did he talk to you about that during the lesson?"

"No, there was no talking at all during the class, apart from when he said I was allowed to join in."

"In which case," said Papa, "I wonder how he managed to find out so much about you...?"

I frowned because I'd been wondering that myself.

"Let's talk about it in the car," said Maman. "Come on."

And we were just about to pile out of the

front door when the phone rang.

"I'll get it!" said Maman, a bit impatiently. She picked up the hall phone. "Hello?" There was a pause and then she smiled and her voice softened. "Hello, Anna. I'll hand you to Jasmeen."

I felt a bit confused for a second, then I realized that Anna must have returned from her tour and picked up my message. I took the phone and was about to blurt out about how I was allowed to do the audition after all, when I realized that I couldn't say that, not with Maman and Papa listening. Otherwise I'd give it away that I'd phoned Anna and asked for her help.

"Hi, Jasmine! I can only talk for a minute because I've just arrived at the stage door, but I wanted to see how everything's going. You sounded so upset in your phone message..."

"You mean you got it? I don't understand how if you're still on tour?"

"When I'm away I check my messages every few days. The moment I got yours I phoned Maurice and explained everything to him and said, 'Help! What can I do? This girl is too good to give up ballet. Who's going to take over when I get too old?' And Maurice said to leave it with him. Then he asked me for your address, but I didn't know it so I told him that your dad worked at the hospital and he said that would do fine. You've got to tell me what's happened, Jasmine! I've been dying to find out."

I didn't know what to say because Maman and Papa were still listening, so I just said, "Thank you very much, Anna."

"Oh, I get it, you can't talk," Anna replied. "Don't worry. Just say *yes* if it's all worked out all right and you're allowed to do the audition."

"Yes."

A big shriek of happiness came down the

phone. The others definitely heard it because they all looked over with surprised expressions on their faces. And Papa raised his eyebrows, but he was smiling.

"Anyway, I've got to go now because I'm going into my dressing room and the line's getting crackly. I'll dance extra specially well tonight, though, now I know that Maurice has worked his magic!"

I wanted to give Anna the biggest thank you in the world, but I knew that would have to wait. So I just gave her another ordinary thank you, and she said, "We'll have a proper talk when I get back."

Then, as we were saying goodbye to each other, I clearly heard the sound of music in the background, and a shiver of happiness ran through me because I was back in my perfect world, and I never, ever had to leave it.

We all piled into the car, but just before we set off Papa turned round to me.

"Anna sounded remarkably happy!" he said, raising his eyebrows.

Rose giggled.

Poppy went pink.

I bit my lip.

And Papa...

Well, Papa winked!

"What a wise man old Maurice is," he said. "Apparently, he sits on all sorts of audition panels as well, you know!" Then he turned back round, exchanged a quick smile with Maman and started driving.

I closed my eyes and remembered the music in the theatre where Anna was about to dance. This was it. My journey to the magical world of professional ballet was truly beginning.

Maybe one day I really would dance with the stars.

❋ ❋ ❋ ❋ ❋

Basic Ballet Positions

First position

Second position

Third position

Fourth position

Fifth position

Ballet words are mostly in French, which makes them more magical. But when you're learning, it's nice to know what they mean too. Here are some of the words that all Miss Coralie's students have to learn:

adage The name for the slow steps in the centre of the room, away from the *barre*.

arabesque A beautiful balance on one leg.

assemblé A jump where the feet come together at the end.

battement dégagé A foot exercise at the *barre* to get beautiful toes.

battement tendu Another foot exercise where you stretch your foot until it points.

chassé A soft smooth slide of the feet.

echappé This one's impossible to describe, but it's like your feet escaping from each other!

fifth position croisé When you are facing, say the *left* corner, with your feet in fifth position, and your front foot is the *right* foot.

fouetté This step is so fast your feet are in a blur! You do it to prepare for *pirouettes*.

grand battement High kick!

jeté A spring where you land on the opposite foot. Rose loves these!

pas de bourrée Tiny little steps to the side, like a mouse.

pas de chat A cat hop from one foot to the other.

plié This is the first step we do in class. You have to bend your knees slowly and make sure your feet are turned right out, with your heels firmly planted on the floor for as long as possible.

port de bras Arm movements, which Poppy is good at.

révérence The curtsey at the end of class.

rond de jambe This is where you make a circle with your leg.

sissonne A scissor step.

sissonne en arrière A scissor step going backwards. This is really hard!

sissonne en avant A scissor step going forwards.

soubresaut A jump off two feet, pointing your feet hard in the air.

temps levé A step and sweep up the other leg, then jump.

turnout You have to stand with your legs and feet and hips all opened out and pointing to the side, not the front. This is the most important thing in ballet that everyone learns right from the start.